Floppy was not well.

He lay on his bed.

"He looks bad," said Kipper.

Biff wanted Floppy to get well.

Kipper was sad.

Mum took Floppy to the vet.

Chip went, too.

Chip looked at the pets.

"I can see six cats," he said.

Floppy just looked at the cats.

He was not well.

The vet looked at Floppy.

"Give him some pills," she said.

Mum took Floppy home.

Floppy had some pills.

Floppy was soon better.